This book belongs to

....

love, Cinders x

Miss Peep x

Alice x

Queen's Pugs x

Q.o.H. ♥

Thumbelina x

For K&E, and for my sisters: the five good fairies – A.L.
For Rebecca – L.B.

PUFFIN BOOKS

UK | USA | Canada | Ireland | Australia
India | New Zealand | South Africa

Puffin Books is part of the Penguin Random House group of companies
whose addresses can be found at global.penguinrandomhouse.com.

www.penguin.co.uk   www.puffin.co.uk   www.ladybird.co.uk

Penguin
Random House
UK

First published by Picture Corgi 2013
This edition published 2022

Text copyright © Abie Longstaff, 2013
Illustrations copyright © Lauren Beard, 2013
The moral right of the author and illustrator has been asserted

Printed in China

The authorized representative in the EEA is
Penguin Random House Ireland, Morrison Chambers,
32 Nassau Street, Dublin D02 YH68

A CIP catalogue record for this book
is available from the British Library

ISBN: 978-0-241-55240-7

All correspondence to:
Puffin Books
Penguin Random House Children's
One Embassy Gardens, 8 Viaduct Gardens
London SW11 7BW

FSC
www.fsc.org
MIX
Paper from
responsible sources
FSC® C018179

THE
FAIRYTALE
HAIRDRESSER
AND
SLEEPING
BEAUTY

Abie Longstaff
&
Lauren Beard

PUFFIN

Kittie Lacey was the best hairdresser in all the land.

Her salon was right in the middle of town and,
because it was so smart and so stylish, everybody went there.

There were high-speed
dryers and beautiful sinks.
It was stocked full of
sweet-smelling shampoos
to suit every kind of hair.
And there was somewhere
comfy to sit and relax.

TROLL BRISTLES

CUT Grass Conditioner

CANDY FLOSS SHAMPOO

Baby bunting hair

Unicorn hair

Zamboo

EWES OF THE WORLD

Mirror Mirror

YOUR CASTLE

The only thing that wasn't stylish at all was the garden.
There were weeds everywhere and giant thorn bushes had taken over.

Kittie sighed. "It'll take a hundred years to fix that mess," she said,
and she closed the back door to hide the garden.

Now, that very morning Prince Florian
came to the salon.
"Hello!" he said. "Any chance of a haircut?"
"Of course," said Kittie, reaching
for the Royal shampoo.

As Kittie combed Prince Florian's
hair, she noticed strange bits of green.
"What have you been doing?" she asked.
The prince laughed. "I'm a garden
designer," he said, "so I always have
leaves in my hair."

Prince Florian showed Kittie pictures of all the gardens he had worked on.

A pigsty makeover

What big flowers!

Grandma's cottage

NO WOLVES

Perfect

My favourite!

"What beautiful gardens," said Kittie. "Do you
have time to design one more? Mine's in a terrible state!"
"Certainly," said the prince. "I'll start tomorrow."

The next day Prince Florian arrived with his trimmers and a big bag of seeds. "This garden's going to be lovely when I'm finished," he said. "I've even brought some of my favourite roses to plant."

He set to work straight away, whistling a tune as he wrestled with gigantic weeds.

Just then the doorbell jangled and into the salon came seven fairies. "Hello!" said Kittie. "I'll be right with you." She smiled at the fairies, but they didn't smile back.

"Oh dear," thought Kittie. "They all look very sad." She took out her prettiest ribbons. "I know how to cheer you up!" she said.

She gave each fairy a fabulous new hairdo.

But even after
Kittie's best efforts
the fairies still
looked upset.

"What's wrong?" Kittie asked, and they burst into tears.
"Oh, Kittie," said Blue Fairy, "we thought coming
here would take our mind off things, but it hasn't."
Kittie made them cups of tea.
"Tell me all about it," she said gently.

"It's our god-daughter, Rose," said Purple Fairy.
"She's fallen asleep and we can't wake her!"
"Goodness!" said Kittie. "What happened?"

When Rose was born, the king and queen held a big party and everyone was invited – everyone except the wicked fairy . . .

We each gave Rose a gift, but just before the last gift was given, the wicked fairy appeared – she was very angry.

The wicked fairy cast an evil spell on Rose. She said that on Rose's eighteenth birthday she would prick her finger on the needle of a spinning wheel and die! As our final gift, we managed to weaken the spell. We said that if Rose did prick her finger, she would not die. Instead, she would fall into a deep sleep, and only the kiss of her true love would awaken her.

The king and queen burned all the spinning wheels throughout the land to keep Rose safe. We thought they had all been destroyed.

ast night was Rose's eighteenth birthday party. All the guests arrived with balloons and presents, but no one could find Rose . . .

Poor Rose had discovered a secret room in the palace, and there, inside, was the last spinning wheel in the land. Rose touched the needle and fell under the spell.

Rose was laid safely in her bed, but before we could find her true love to break the spell, the wicked fairy appeared. She put everyone to sleep, covering the palace with an enchanted thicket of thorns so that nobody could get to Rose ~ we only just escaped in time!

HAPPY 18TH BIRTHDAY

"Oh no!" cried Kittie. "How terrible!" Green Fairy's eyes filled with tears.
"Poor Rose," she said. "Only a kiss from her true love will wake her up."
"But we don't know who her true love is!" sobbed Pink Fairy in despair.
"And we'll never cut through those thorns!" Yellow Fairy cried.

"Hmm," said Kittie,
"I think I know someone who could help . . ."

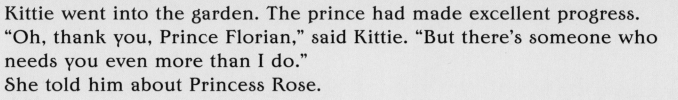

Kittie went into the garden. The prince had made excellent progress.
"Oh, thank you, Prince Florian," said Kittie. "But there's someone who
needs you even more than I do."
She told him about Princess Rose.

"I know that garden," said the prince.
"I designed it only last month. And
I know Rose too! She helped me with
all the flower beds. She's lovely."
He blushed. "We've got to help her!"

They sped to the palace as fast as they could. But they could hardly see it behind the enchanted thicket and the ferocious weeds that had grown among the thorns.

Kittie got out her sharpest scissors and Prince Florian used his clippers . . .

Together they hacked away at the thicket. It was hard work!

The thorns were enormous. The tendrils tangled round their legs. And some of the snapdragons and toadstools were very cross indeed. The friends battled on and finally cut a path to the palace gate.

Inside the palace everything was very quiet.
Everything was very still.

Kittie and Prince Florian crossed the
courtyard to reach a twisting staircase.
"Our Sleeping Beauty is up there," said the fairies.

Up and up they climbed.

Finally, at the top of the tallest tower they found a lovely princess lying fast asleep.

"Oh, Rose!" cried Prince Florian.
He ran straight to her side and took
her hand in his. "Poor Rose!"

The fairies opened up *The Big Book of Princes.*
"Which one could be her true love?" they wondered.

Prince Handsome

Prince Charming

Prince Brave

Prince Rich

"He must be one of these," said Red Fairy.

Kittie looked all around Rose's room.
"Hang on," she said. "I have a feeling I know who her true love is!"

Kittie knelt by the prince.
"Prince Florian," she said, "Rose is
a special friend of yours, isn't she?"
"Yes," he sniffed. "Rose loves
gardens just like I do.

We would often sit and weed together.
She would sing and I would whistle . . .

She has a lovely voice," he said sadly. "Oh, Rose!"
In despair the prince leaned over and kissed his true love.
For a moment there was silence. Then Rose's eyelashes
fluttered. She opened her eyes and sat up.

"Rose!" the fairies cried. "You're awake! The spell is broken!"

But just then there was
an awful cackle . . .

. . . it was
the wicked fairy!

"Nooo!" she screeched, taking out her
wand and shooting a sleeping spell
straight towards Rose.

As quick as she could, Kittie pulled out her hand mirror. She held it up high in the air. The sleeping spell bounced off and . . .

WHOOSH!

. . . it hit the wicked fairy!

Down fell the wicked fairy into a deep sleep. "Wow!" said Rose. "She snores really loudly." The prince laughed and swept her up into his arms.

For the next few weeks everyone was very busy helping to tidy the palace. Kittie, Florian and Rose were very busy fixing the garden . . .

And the wicked fairy was very busy sleeping.

Soon everything was ready for an extra-special day . . .

. . . the day when Princess Rose married her true love, Prince Florian. Their parents couldn't be more proud. The seven fairies were over the moon! And of course Kittie was very happy too.

But what about Kittie's garden?

Nowadays it looks just as stylish
as her salon!